MY SPARKLE

By Cheryl Elam

Balboa Press books may be ordered through booksellers or by contacting:

Balboa Press
A Division of Hay House
1663 Liberty Drive
Bloomington, IN 47403
www.balboapress.com
1 (877) 407-4847

Interior Image Credit: Nadia Hussain

ISBN: 978-1-9822-3385-3 (sc)
ISBN: 978-1-9822-3386-0 (e)

Library of Congress Control Number: 2019912659

Print information available on the last page.

Balboa Press rev. date: 08/31/2019

BALBOA
PRESS
A DIVISION OF HAY HOUSE

MY
SPARKLE

I am walking, walking down a path.
I look, but for as far as I can
see, there is nothing.
Everything looks the same.

There is no direction, no guidance.
Yet, I continue walking.
Where this path will lead, I cannot tell.
Still, it beckons me onward.

I walk for miles, over hills,
through valleys,
around countless twists and turns.
One step in front of the other,
toward a destination unknown.

But what's this?
As I round the next corner,
I catch a glimpse of something.
There's a glimmer.
Something is out there!

Curiosity and excitement take hold!
My pace quickens!
I head toward this SPARKLE
in the distance.
It keeps me walking.

I get intermittent glimpses
of this SPARKLE.
It's way out there.
It's far away now, but it is
drawing me toward it.

OH NO!!!
Where did it go?
I can't see it anymore!
What happened to MY SPARKLE?

I must find it!
I must keep looking for it!
I continue onward.
Over more hills and
through more valleys.
Tracking endless miles down this path.

I rush toward it! Determined not to lose it this time. It is there!

It is starting to take shape
as I close in on it.
I can see where I am headed now!
I can see my destination!

WHOA!!!
What is that?
Up there in the path?
It's a HUGE canyon!!!
It's preventing me from
getting to MY SPARKLE!
What am I going to do?

I've come so far,
and now, I won't be able to
make it to MY SPARKLE.
The canyon is SO DEEP,
and SO WIDE,
How can I possibly
get across it?

NO!!!

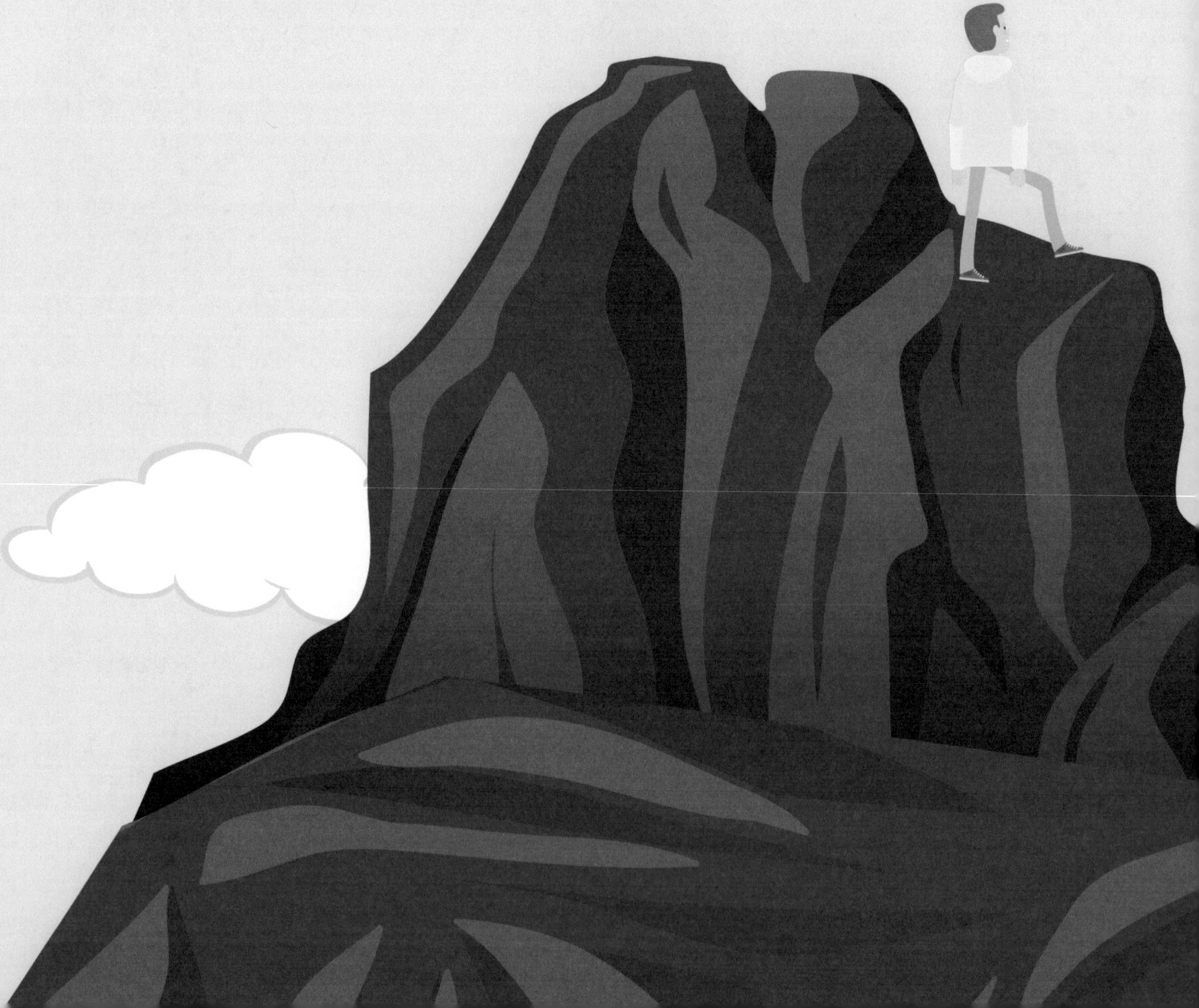

I must take a leap of faith!
I am going to jump across it!
Yeah, that's what
I'm going to do!

Deep breath, eyes closed,
Pause...
JUST DO IT!!!
Okay! Okay!
1, 2, 3... Here I go!
JUMP!!!

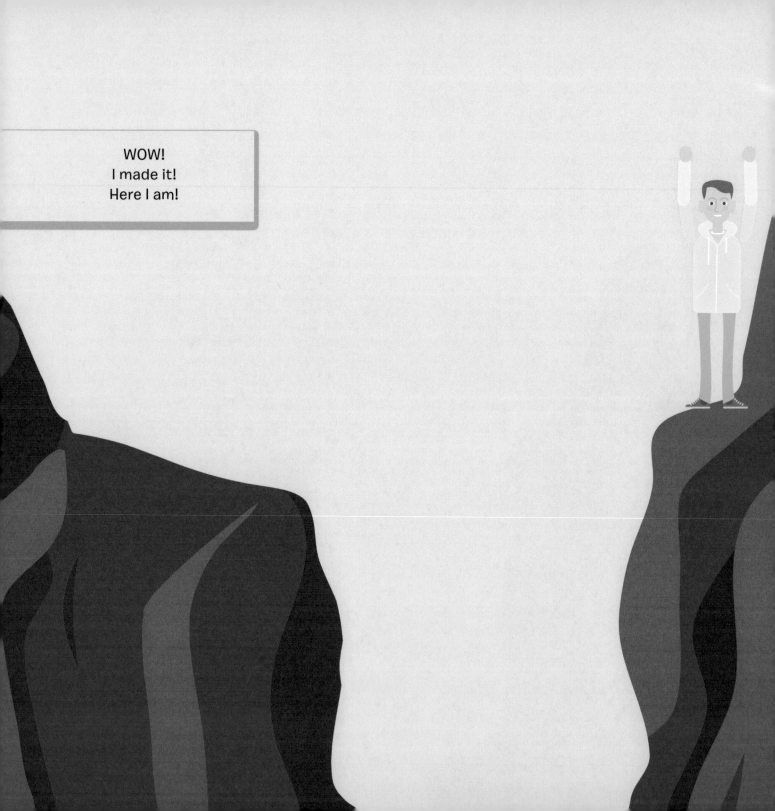

I made it to MY SPARKLE!
My destiny!
It's everything I ever
dreamed of!
I am so happy!

Um, it's funny.
That canyon doesn't look nearly as
deep or as wide from this side.
It just looks like a rut
in the road now.

Come to think of it,

I've had MY SPARKLE with me all along.

It has always been there.

It had just been pushed down
and buried so deep,

that I couldn't see it's light anymore.

BUT NOT NOW!

Now MY SPARKLE is shining bright
for the whole world to see!

And I will never let the beautiful light of

MY SPARKLE

go out again!

EMPOWERMENT MESSAGE

YOUR SPARKLE

You have special gifts and talents that God has given just to you. They make you unique in all the universe.

They are a reflection of your soul, your inner beauty, the true you. They will help you to do wonderful things with your life and for others.

When you let Your Sparkle shine, your potential is limitless. You can accomplish anything!

Don't ever let anyone or anything put Your Sparkle out. Be true to who you are, and let Your Sparkle shine for the whole world to see!

Printed in the United States
By Bookmasters